A WORLD
is Born

A WORLD
is Born
LEIGH BRACKETT

ÆGYPAN PRESS

Special thanks to Greg Weeks, Joel Schlosberg, and the On-line Distributed Proofreading Team (which can be found at http://www.pgdp.net).

This story first appeared in the July, 1941, issue of *Comet* magazine.

A World is Born
A publication of
ÆGYPAN PRESS

www.aegypan.com

The first ripples of blue fire touched Dio's men. Bolts of it fastened on gun-butts, and knuckles. Men screamed and fell. Jill cried out as he tore silver ornaments from her dress.

Mel Gray flung down his hoe with a sudden tigerish fierceness and stood erect. Tom Ward, working beside him, glanced at Gray's Indianesque profile, the youth of it hardened by war and the hells of the Eros prison blocks.

A quick flash of satisfaction crossed Ward's dark eyes. Then he grinned and said mockingly.

"Hell of a place to spend the rest of your life, ain't it?"

Mel Gray stared with slitted blue eyes down the valley. The huge sun of Mercury seared his naked body. Sweat channeled the dust on his skin. His throat ached with thirst. And the bitter landscape mocked him more than Wade's dark face.

"The rest of my life," he repeated softly. "The rest of my life!"

He was twenty-eight.

Wade spat in the damp black earth. "You ought to be glad — helping the unfortunate, building a haven for the derelict. . . ."

"Shut up!" Fury rose in Gray, hotter than the boiling springs that ran from the Sunside to water the valleys.

He hated Mercury. He hated John Moulton and his daughter Jill, who had conceived this plan of building a new world for the destitute and desperate veterans of the Second Interplanetary War.

"I've had enough 'unselfish service'," he whispered. "I'm serving myself from now on."

Escape. That was all he wanted. Escape from these stifling valleys, from the snarl of the wind in the barren crags that towered higher than Everest into airless space. Escape from the surveillance of the twenty guards, the forced companionship of the ninety-nine other veteran-convicts.

Wade poked at the furrows between the sturdy hybrid tubers. "It ain't possible, kid. Not even for 'Duke' Gray, the 'light-fingered genius who held the Interstellar Police at a standstill for five years'." He laughed. "I read your publicity."

Gray stroked slow, earth-stained fingers over his sleek cap of yellow hair. "You think so?" he asked softly.

Dio the Martian came down the furrow, his lean, wiry figure silhouetted against the upper panorama of the valley; the neat rows of vegetables and the green riot of Venusian wheat, dotted with toiling men and their friendly guards.

Dio's green, narrowed eyes studied Gray's hard face.

"What's the matter, Gray? Trying to start something?"

"Suppose I were?" asked Gray silkily. Dio was the unofficial leader of the convict-veterans. There was about his thin body and hatchet face some of the grim determination that had made the Martians cling to their dying world and bring life to it again.

"You volunteered, like the rest of us," said the Martian. "Haven't you the guts to stick it?"

"The hell I volunteered! The IPA sent me. And what's it to you?"

"Only this." Dio's green eyes were slitted and ugly. "You've only been here a month. The rest of us came nearly a year ago — because we wanted to. We've worked like slaves, because we wanted to. In three weeks the crops will be in. The Moulton Project will be self-supporting. Moulton will get his permanent charter, and we'll be on our way.

"There are ninety-nine of us, Gray, who want the Moulton Project to succeed. We know that that louse Caron of Mars doesn't want it to, since pitchblende was discovered. We don't know whether you're working for him or not, but you're a troublemaker.

"There isn't to be any trouble, Gray. We're not giving the Interplanetary Prison Authority any excuse to revoke its decision and give Caron of Mars a free hand here. We'll see to anyone who tries it. Understand?"

*M*el Gray took one slow step forward, but Ward's sharp, "Stow it! A guard," stopped him. The Martian worked back up the furrow. The guard, reassured, strolled back up the valley, squinting at the jagged streak of pale-grey sky that was going black as low clouds formed, only a few hundred feet above the copper cables that ran from cliff to cliff high over their heads.

"Another storm," growled Ward. "It gets worse as Mercury enters perihelion. Lovely world, ain't it?"

"Why did you volunteer?" asked Gray, picking up his hoe.

Ward shrugged. "I had my reasons."

Gray voiced the question that had troubled him since his transfer. "There were hundreds on the waiting list to replace the man who died. Why did they send me, instead?"

"Some fool blunder," said Ward carelessly. And then, in the same casual tone, "You mean it, about escaping?"

Gray stared at him. "What's it to you?"

Ward moved closer. "I can help you?"

A stab of mingled hope and wary suspicion transfixed Gray's heart. Ward's dark face grinned briefly into his, with a flash of secretive black eyes, and Gray was conscious of distrust.

"What do you mean, help me?"

Dio was working closer, watching them. The first growl of thunder rattled against the cliff faces. It was dark now, the pink flames of the Dark-side aurora visible beyond the valley mouth.

"I've got — connections," returned Ward cryptically. "Interested?"

Gray hesitated. There was too much he couldn't understand. Moreover, he was a lone wolf. Had been since the Second Interplanetary War wrenched him from the quiet backwater of his country home an eternity of eight years before and hammered him into hardness — a cynic who trusted nobody and nothing but Mel 'Duke' Gray.

"If you have connections," he said slowly, "why don't you use 'em yourself?"

"I got my reasons." Again that secretive grin. "But it's no hide off you, is it? All you want is to get away."

That was true. It would do no harm to hear what Ward had to say.

Lightning burst overhead, streaking down to be caught and grounded by the copper cables. The livid flare showed Dio's face, hard with worry and determination. Gray nodded.

"Tonight, then," whispered Ward. "In the barracks."

Out from the cleft where Mel Gray worked, across the flat plain of rock stripped naked by the wind that raved across it, lay the deep valley that sheltered the heart of the Moulton Project.

Hot springs joined to form a steaming river. Vegetation grew savagely under the huge sun. The air, kept at almost constant temperature by the blanketing effect of the hot springs, was stagnant and heavy.

But up above, high over the copper cables that crossed every valley where men ventured, the eternal wind of Mercury screamed and snarled between the naked cliffs.

Three concrete domes crouched on the valley floor, housing barracks, tool-shops, kitchens, store-houses, and executive quarters, connected by underground passages. Beside the smallest dome, joined to it by a heavily barred tunnel, was an insulated hangar, containing the only space ship on Mercury.

In the small dome, John Moulton leaned back from a pile of reports, took a pinch of Martian snuff, sneezed lustily, and said.

"Jill, I think we've done it."

The grey-eyed, black-haired young woman turned from the quartzite window through which she had been watching the gathering storm overhead. The thunder from other valleys reached them as a dim barrage which, at this time of Mercury's year, was never still.

"I don't know," she said. "It seems that nothing can happen now, and yet. . . . It's been too easy."

"Easy!" snorted Moulton. "We've broken our backs fighting these valleys. And our nerves, fighting time. But we've licked 'em!"

He rose, shaggy grey hair tousled, grey eyes alight.

"I told the IPA those men weren't criminals. And I was right. They can't deny me the charter now. No matter how much Caron of Mars would like to get his claws on this radium."

He took Jill by the shoulders and shook her, laughing.

"Three weeks, girl, that's all. First crops ready for harvest, first pay-ore coming out of the mines. In three weeks my permanent charter will have to be granted, according to agreement, and then. . . .

"Jill," he added solemnly, "we're seeing the birth of a world."

"That's what frightens me." Jill glanced upward as the first flare of lightning struck down, followed by a crash of thunder that shook the dome.

"So much can happen at a birth. I wish the three weeks were over!"

"Nonsense, girl! What could possibly happen?"

She looked at the copper cables, burning with the electricity running along them, and thought of the one hundred and twenty-two souls in that narrow Twilight Belt — with the fierce heat of the Sunside before them and the spatial cold of the Shadow side at their backs, fighting against wind and storm and heat to build a world to replace the ones the War had taken from them.

"So much could happen," she whispered. "An accident, an escape. . . ."

The inter-dome telescreen buzzed its signal. Jill, caught in a queer mood of premonition, went to it.

The face of Dio the Martian appeared on the screen, still wet and dirty from the storm-soaked fields, disheveled from his battle across the plain in the chaotic winds.

"I want to see you, Miss Moulton," he said. "There's something funny I think you ought to know."

"Of course," said Jill, and met her father's eyes. "I think we'll see, now, which one of us is right."

*T*he barracks were quiet, except for the mutter of distant thunder and the heavy breathing of exhausted men. Tom Ward crouched in the darkness by Mel Gray's bunk.

"You ain't gonna go soft at the last minute, are you?" he whispered. "Because I can't afford to take chances."

"Don't worry," Gray returned grimly. "What's your proposition?"

"I can give you the combination to the lock of the hangar passage. All you have to do is get into Moulton's office, where the passage door is, and go to it. The ship's a two-seater. You can get her out of the valley easy."

Gray's eyes narrowed in the dark. "What's the catch?"

"There ain't none. I swear it."

"Look, Ward. I'm no fool. Who's behind this, and why?"

"That don't make no difference. All you want . . . *ow!*"

Gray's fingers had fastened like steel claws on his wrist.

"I get it, now," said Gray slowly. "That's why I was sent here. Somebody wanted me to make trouble for Moulton." His fingers tightened agonizingly, and his voice sank to a slow drawl.

"I don't like being a pawn in somebody else's chess game."

"Okay, okay! It ain't my fault. Lemme go." Ward rubbed his bruised wrist. "Sure, somebody — I ain't sayin' who — sent you here, knowin' you'd want to escape. I'm here to help you. You get free, I get paid, the Big Boy gets what he wants. Okay?"

Gray was silent, scowling in the darkness. Then he said.

"All right. I'll take a chance."

"Then listen. You tell Moulton you have a complaint. I'll. . . ."

Light flooded the dark as the door clanged open. Ward leaped like a startled rabbit, but the light speared him, held him. Ward felt a pulse of excitement beat up in him.

The long ominous shadows of the guards raised elongated guns. The barracks stirred and muttered, like a vast aviary waking.

"Ward and Gray," said one of the guards. "Moulton wants you."

Gray rose from his bunk with the lithe, delicate grace of a cat. The monotony of sleep and labor was ended. Something had broken. Life was once again a moving thing.

*J*ohn Moulton sat behind the untidy desk. Dio the Martian sat grimly against the wall. There was a guard beside him, watching.

Mel Gray noted all this as he and Ward came in. But his cynical blue eyes went beyond, to a door with a ponderous combination lock. Then they were attracted by something else — the tall, slim figure standing against the black quartz panes of the far wall.

It was the first time he had seen Jill Moulton. She looked the perfect sober apostle of righteousness he'd learned to mock. And then he saw the soft cluster of black curls, the curve of her throat above the dark dress, the red lips that balanced her determined jaw and direct grey eyes.

Moulton spoke, his shaggy head hunched between his shoulders.

"Dio tells me that you, Gray, are not a volunteer."

"Tattletale," said Gray. He was gauging the distance to the hangar door, the positions of the guards, the time it would take to spin out the combination. And he knew he couldn't do it.

"What were you and Ward up to when the guards came?"

"I couldn't sleep," said Gray amiably. "He was telling me bedtime stories." Jill Moulton was lovely, he couldn't deny that. Lovely, but not soft. She gave him an idea.

Moulton's jaw clamped. "Cut the comedy, Gray. Are you working for Caron of Mars?"

Caron of Mars, chairman of the board of the Interplanetary Prison Authority. Dio had mentioned him. Gray smiled in understanding. Caron of Mars had sent him, Gray, to Mercury. Caron of Mars was helping him, through Ward, to escape. Caron of Mars wanted Mercury for his own purposes — and he could have it.

"In a manner of speaking, Mr. Moulton," he said gravely, "Caron of Mars is working for me."

He caught Ward's sharp hiss of remonstrance. Then Jill Moulton stepped forward.

"Perhaps he doesn't understand what he's doing, Father." Her eyes met Gray's. "You want to escape, don't you?"

Gray studied her, grinning as the slow rose flushed her skin, the corners of her mouth tightening with anger.

"Go on," he said. "You have a nice voice."

Her eyes narrowed, but she held her temper.

"You must know what that would mean, Gray. There are thousands of veterans in the prisons now. Their offenses are mostly trivial, but the Prison Authority can't let them go, because they have no jobs, no homes, no money.

"The valleys here are fertile. There are mines rich in copper and pitchblende. The men have a chance for a home and a job, a part in building a new world. We hope to make Mercury an independent, self-governing member of the League of Worlds."

"With the Moultons as rulers, of course," Gray murmured.

"If they want us," answered Jill, deliberately missing the point. "Do you think you have the right to destroy all we've worked for?"

Gray was silent. Rather grimly, she went on.

"Caron of Mars would like to see us defeated. He didn't care about Mercury before radium was discovered. But now he'd like to turn it into a prison mining community, with convict labor, leasing mine grants to corporations and cleaning up big fortunes for himself and his associates.

"Any trouble here will give him an excuse to say that we've failed, that the Project is a menace to the Solar System. If you try to escape, you wreck everything we've done. If you don't tell the truth, you may cost thousands of men their futures.

"Do you understand? Will you cooperate?"

Gray said evenly, "I'm my own keeper, now. My brother will have to take care of himself."

It was ridiculously easy, she was so earnest, so close to him. He had a brief kaleidoscope of impressions — Ward's sullen bewilderment, Moulton's angry roar, Dio's jerky rise to his feet as the guards grabbed for their guns.

Then he had his hands around her slim, firm throat, her body pressed close to his, serving as a shield against bullets.

"Don't be rash," he told them all quietly. "I can break her neck quite easily, if I have to. Ward, unlock that door."

In utter silence, Ward darted over and began to spin the dial. At last he said, "Okay, c'mon."

Gray realized that he was sweating. Jill was like warm, rigid marble in his hands. And he had another idea.

"I'm going to take the girl as a hostage," he announced. "If I get safely away, she'll be turned loose, her health and virtue still intact. Good night."

The clang of the heavy door had a comforting sound behind them.

*T*he ship was a commercial job, fairly slow but sturdy. Gray strapped Jill Moulton into one of the bucket seats in the control room and then checked the fuel and air gauges. The tanks were full.

"What about you?" he said to Ward. "You can't go back."

"Nah. I'll have to go with you. Warm her up, Duke, while I open the dome."

He darted out. Gray set the atmosphere motors idling. The dome slid open, showing the flicker of the auroras, where areas of intense heat and cold set up atmospheric tension by rapid fluctuation of adjoining air masses.

Mercury, cutting the vast magnetic field of the Sun in an eccentric orbit, tortured by the daily change from blistering heat to freezing cold in the thin atmosphere, was a powerful generator of electricity.

Ward didn't come back.

Swearing under his breath, tense for the sound of pursuit in spite of the girl, Gray went to look. Out beyond the hangar, he saw a figure running.

Running hard up into the narrowing cleft of the valley, where natural galleries in the rock of Mercury led to the places where the copper cables were anchored, and farther, into the unexplored mystery of the caves.

Gray scowled, his arrogant Roman profile hard against the flickering aurora. Then he slammed the lock shut.

The ship roared out into the tearing winds of the plain. Gray cut in his rockets and blasted up, into the airless dark among the high peaks.

Jill Moulton hadn't moved or spoken.

Gray snapped on the space radio, leaving his own screen dark. Presently he picked up signals in a code he didn't know.

"Listen," he said. "I knew there was some reason for Ward's running out on me."

His Indianesque face hardened. "So that's the game! They want to make trouble for you by letting me escape and then make themselves heroes by bringing me in, preferably dead.

"They've got ships waiting to get me as soon as I clear Mercury, and they're getting stand-by instructions from somebody on the ground. The somebody that Ward was making for."

Jill's breath made a small hiss. "Somebody's near the Project. . . ."

Gray snapped on his transmitter.

"Duke Gray, calling all ships off Mercury. Will the flagship of your reception committee please come in?"

His screen flickered to life. A man's face appeared — the middle-aged, soft-fleshed, almost stickily innocent face of one of the Solar Systems greatest crusaders against vice and crime.

Jill Moulton gasped. "Caron of Mars!"

"Ward gave the game away," said Gray gently. "Too bad."

The face of Caron of Mars never changed expression. But behind those flesh-hooded eyes was a cunning brain, working at top speed.

"I have a passenger," Gray went on. "Miss Jill Moulton. I'm responsible for her safety, and I'd hate to have her inconvenienced."

The tip of a pale tongue flicked across Caron's pale lips.

"That is a pity," he said, with the intonation of a preaching minister. "But I cannot stop the machinery set in motion. . . ."

"And besides," finished Gray acidly, "you think that if Jill Moulton dies with me, it'll break John Moulton so he won't fight you at all."

His lean hand poised on the switch.

"All right, you putrid flesh-tub. Try and catch us!"

The screen went dead. Gray hunched over the controls. If he could get past them, lose himself in the glare of the Sun. . . .

He looked aside at the stony-faced girl beside him. She was studying him contemptuously out of hard grey eyes.

"How," she said slowly, "can you be such a callous swine?"

"Callous?" He controlled the quite unreasonable anger that rose in him. "Not at all. The war taught me that if I didn't look out for myself, no one would."

"And yet you must have started out a human being."

He laughed.

The ship burst into searing sunlight. The Sunside of Mercury blazed below them. Out toward the velvet dark of space the side of a waiting ship flashed burning silver.

Even as he watched, the flare of its rockets arced against the blackness. They had been sighted.

Gray's practiced eye gauged the stranger's speed against his own, and he cursed softly. Abruptly he wheeled the ship and started down again, cutting his rockets as the shadow swallowed them. The ship was eerily silent, dropping with a rising scream as the atmosphere touched the hull.

"What are you going to do?" asked Jill almost too quietly.

He didn't answer. Maneuvering the ship on velocity between those stupendous pinnacles took all his attention. Caron, at least, couldn't follow him in the dark without exhaust flares as guides.

They swept across the wind-torn plain, into the mouth of the valley where Gray had worked, braking hard to a stop under the cables.

"You might have got past them," said Jill.

"One chance in a hundred."

Her mouth twisted. "Afraid to take it?"

He smiled harshly. "I haven't yet reached the stage where I kill women. You'll be safe here — the men will find you in the morning. I'm going back, alone."

"Safe!" she said bitterly. "For what? No matter what happens, the Project is ruined."

"Don't worry," he told her brutally. "You'll find some other way to make a living."

Her eyes blazed. "You think that's all its means to us? Just money and power?" She whispered, "I hope they kill you, Duke Gray!"

*H*e rose lazily and opened the air lock, then turned and freed her. And, sharply, the valley was bathed in a burst of light.

"Damn!" Gray picked up the sound of air motors overhead. "They must have had infra-red search beams. Well, that does it. We'll have to run for it, since this bus isn't armed."

With eerie irrelevancy, the teleradio buzzed. At this time of night, after the evening storms, some communication was possible.

Gray had a hunch. He opened the switch, and the face of John Moulton appeared on the screen. It was white and oddly still.

"Our guards saw your ship cross the plain," said Moulton quietly. "The men of the Project, led by Dio, are coming for you. I sent them, because I have decided that the life of my daughter is less important than the lives of many thousands of people.

"I appeal to you, Gray, to let her go. Her life won't save you. And it's very precious to me."

Caron's ship swept over, low above the cables, and the grinding concussion of a bomb lifted the ship, hurled it down with the stern end twisted to uselessness. The screen went dead.

Gray caught the half stunned girl. "I wish to heaven I could get rid of you!" he grated. "And I don't know why I don't!"

But she was with him when he set out down the valley, making for the cliff caves, up where the copper cables were anchored.

Caron's ship, a fast, small fighter, wheeled between the cliffs and turned back. Gray dropped flat, holding the girl down. Bombs pelted them with dirt and uprooted vegetables, started fires in the wheat. The pilot found a big enough break in the cables and came in for a landing.

Gray was up and running again. He knew the way into the explored galleries. From there on, it was anybody's guess.

Caron was brazen enough about it. The subtle way had failed. Now he was going all out. And he was really quite safe. With the broken cables to act as conductors, the first thunderstorm would obliterate all proof of his activities in this valley. Mercury, because of its high electrical potential, was cut off from communication with other worlds. Moulton, even if he had knowledge of what went on, could not send for help.

Gray wondered briefly what Caron intended to do in case he, Gray, made good his escape. That outpost in the main valley, for which Ward had been heading, wasn't kept for fun. Besides, Caron was too smart to have only one string to his bow.

Shouts, the spatter of shots around them. The narrow trail loomed above. Gray sent the girl scrambling up.

The sun burst up over the high peaks, leaving the black shadow of the valley still untouched. Caron's ship roared off. But six of its crew came after Gray and Jill Moulton.

*T*he chill dark of the tunnel mouth swallowed them. Keeping right to avoid the great copper posts that held the cables, strung through holes drilled in the solid rock of the gallery's outer wall, Gray urged the girl along.

The cleft his hand was searching for opened. Drawing the girl inside, around a jutting shoulder, he stopped, listening.

Footsteps echoed outside, grew louder, swept by. There was no light. But the steps were too sure to have been made in the dark.

"Infra-red torches and goggles," Gray said tersely, "You see, but your quarry doesn't. Useful gadget. Come on."

"But where? What are you going to do?"

"Escape, girl. Remember? They smashed my ship. But there must be another one on Mercury. I'm going to find it."

"I don't understand."

"You probably never will. Here's where I leave you. That Martian Galahad will be along any minute. He'll take you home."

Her voice came soft and puzzled through the dark.

"I don't understand you, Gray. You wouldn't risk my life. Yet you're turning me loose, knowing that I might save you, knowing that I'll hunt you down if I can. I thought you were a hardened cynic."

"What makes you think I'm not?"

"If you were, you'd have kicked me out the waste tubs of the ship and gone on. You'd never have turned back."

"I told you," he said roughly, "I don't kill women." He turned away, but her harsh chuckle followed him.

"You're a fool, Gray. You've lost truth — and you aren't even true to your lie."

He paused, in swift anger. Voices the sound of running men, came up from the path. He broke into a silent run, following the dying echoes of Caron's men.

"Run, Gray!" cried Jill. "Because we're coming after you!"

The tunnels, ancient blowholes for the volcanic gases that had tortured Mercury with the raising of the titanic mountains, sprawled in a labyrinthine network through those same vast peaks. Only the galleries lying next the valleys had been explored. Man's habitation on Mercury had been too short.

Gray could hear Caron's men circling about through connecting tunnels, searching. It proved what he had already guessed. He was taking a desperate chance. But the way back was closed — and he was used to taking chances.

The geography of the district was clear in his mind — the valley he had just left and the main valley, forming an obtuse angle with the apex out on the wind-torn plain and a double range of mountains lying out between the sides of the triangle.

Somewhere there was a passage through those peaks. Somewhere there was a landing place, and ten to one there was a ship on it. Caron would never have left his men stranded, on the off chance that they might be discovered and used in evidence against him.

The men now hunting him knew their way through the tunnels, probably with the aid of markings that fluoresced under infra-red light. They were going to take him through, too.

They were coming closer. He waited far up in the main gallery, in the mouth of a side tunnel. Now, behind them, he could hear Dio's men. The noise of Caron's outfit stopped, then began again, softly.

Gray smiled, his sense of humor pleased. He tensed, waiting.

*T*he rustle of cloth, the furtive creak of leather, the clink of metal equipment. Heavy breathing. Somebody whispered,

"Who the hell's that back there?"

"Must be men from the Project. We'd better hurry."

"We've got to find that damned Gray first," snapped the first voice grimly. "Caron'll burn us if we don't."

Gray counted six separate footsteps, trying to allow for the echoes. When he was sure the last man was by, he stepped out. The noise of Dio's hunt was growing — there must be a good many of them.

Covered by their own echoes, he stole up on the men ahead. His groping hand brushed gently against the clothing of the last man in the group. Gauging his distance swiftly, he went into action.

One hand fastened over the fellow's mouth. The other, holding a good-sized rock, struck down behind the ear. Gray eased the body down with scarcely a sound.

Their uniforms, he had noticed, were not too different from his prison garb. In a second he had stripped goggles, cap, and gun-belt from the body, and was striding after the others.

They moved like five eerie shadows now, in the queer light of the leader's lamp. Small fluorescent markings guided them. The last man grunted over his shoulder,

"What happened to you?"

"Stumbled," whispered Gray tersely, keeping his head down. A whisper is a good disguise for the voice. The other nodded.

"Don't straggle. No fun, getting lost in here."

The leader broke in. "We'll circle again. Be careful of that Project bunch — they'll be using ordinary light. And be quiet!"

They went, through connecting passages. The noise of Dio's party grew ominously loud. Abruptly, the leader swore.

"Caron or no Caron, he's gone. And we'd better go, too."

He turned off, down a different tunnel, and Gray heaved a sigh of relief, remembering the body he'd left in the open. For a time the noise of their pursuers grew remote. And then, suddenly, there was an echoing clamor of footsteps, and the glare of torches on the wall of a cross-passage ahead.

Voices came to Gray, distorted by the rock vaults.

"I'm sure I heard them, just then." It was Jill's voice.

"Yeah." That was Dio. "The trouble is, where?"

The footsteps halted. Then, "Let's try this passage. We don't want to get too far into this maze."

Caron's leader blasphemed softly and dodged into a side tunnel. The man next to Gray stumbled and cried out with pain as he struck the wall, and a shout rose behind them.

The leader broke into a run, twisting, turning, diving into the maze of smaller tunnels. The sounds of pursuit faded, were lost in the tomblike silence of the caves. One of the men laughed.

"We sure lost 'em!"

"Yeah," said the leader. "We lost 'em, all right." Gray caught the note of panic in his voice. "We lost the markers, too."

"You mean. . .?"

"Yeah. Turning off like that did it. Unless we can find that marked tunnel, we're sunk!"

Gray, silent in the shadows, laughed a bitter, ironic laugh.

*T*hey went on, stumbling down endless black halls, losing all track of branching corridors, straining to catch the first glint of saving light. Once or twice they caught the echoes of Dio's party, and knew that they, too, were lost and wandering.

Then, quite suddenly, they came out into a vast gallery, running like a subway tube straight to left and right. A wind tore down it, hot as a draft from the burning gates of Hell.

It was a moment before anyone grasped the significance of that wind. Then someone shouted,

"We're saved! All we have to do is walk against it!"

They turned left, almost running in the teeth of that searing blast. And Gray began to notice a peculiar thing.

The air was charged with electricity. His clothing stiffened and crackled. His hair crawled on his head. He could see the faint discharges of sparks from his companions.

Whether it was the effect of the charged air, or the reaction from the nervous strain of the past hours, Mel Gray began to be afraid.

Weary to exhaustion, they struggled on against the burning wind. And then they blundered out into a cave, huge as a cathedral, lighted by a queer, uncertain bluish light.

Gray caught the sharp smell of ozone. His whole body was tingling with electric tension. The bluish light seemed to be in indeterminate lumps scattered over the rocky floor. The rush of the wind under that tremendous vault was terrifying.

They stopped, Gray keeping to the background. Now was the time to evade his unconscious helpers. The moment they reached daylight, he'd be discovered.

Soft-footed as a cat, he was already hidden among the heavy shadows of the fluted walls when, he heard the voices.

They came from off to the right, a confused shout of men under fearful strain, growing louder and louder, underscored with the tramp of footsteps. Lights blazed suddenly in the cathedral dark, and from the mouth of a great tunnel some hundred yards away, the men of the Project poured into the cave.

And then, sharp and high and unexpected, a man screamed.

*T*he lumps of blue light were moving. And a man had died. He lay on the rock, his flesh blackened jelly, with a rope of glowing light running from the metal of his gun butt to the metal buttons on his cap.

All across the vast floor of that cavern the slow, eerie ripple of motion grew. The scattered lumps melted and flowed together, converging in wavelets of blue flame upon the men.

The answer came to Gray. Those things were some form of energy-life, born of the tremendous electric tensions on Mercury. Like all electricity, they were attracted to metal.

In a sudden frenzy of motion, he ripped off his metal-framed goggles, his cap and gun-belt. The Moultons forbade metal because of the danger of lightning, and his boots were made of rubber, so he felt reasonably safe, but a tense fear ran in prickling waves across his skin.

Guns began to bark, their feeble thunder all but drowned in the vast rush of the wind. Bullets struck the oncoming waves of light with no more effect than the eruption of a shower of sparks. Gray's attention, somehow, was riveted on Jill, standing with Dio at the head of her men.

She wore ordinary light slippers, having been dressed only for indoors. And there were silver ornaments at waist and throat.

He might have escaped, then, quite unnoticed. Instead, for a reason even he couldn't understand, he ran for Jill Moulton.

The first ripples of blue fire touched the ranks of Dio's men. Bolts of it leaped upward to fasten upon gun-butts and the buckles of the cartridge belts. Men screamed, fell, and died.

An arm of the fire licked out, driving in behind Dio and the girl. The guns of Caron's four remaining men were silent, now.

Gray leaped over that hissing electric surf, running toward Jill. A hungry worm of light reared up, searching for Dio's gun. Gray's hand swept it down, to be instantly buried in a mass of glowing ropes. Dio's hatchet face snarled at him in startled anger.

Jill cried out as Gray tore the silver ornaments from her dress. "Throw down the guns!" he yelled. "It's metal they want!"

He heard his name shouted by men torn momentarily from their own terror. Dio cried, "Shoot him!" A few bullets whined past, but their immediate fear spoiled both aim and attention.

Gray caught up Jill and began to run, toward the tube from which the wind howled in the cave. Behind him, grimly, Dio followed.

The electric beasts didn't notice him. His insulated feet trampled through them, buried to the ankle in living flame, feeling queer tenuous bodies break and reform.

The wind met them like a physical barrier at the tunnel mouth. Gray put Jill down. The wind strangled him. He tore off his coat and wrapped it over the girl's head, using his shirt over his own. Jill, her black curls whipped straight, tried to fight back past him, and he saw Dio coming, bent double against the wind.

He saw something else. Something that made him grab Jill and point, his flesh crawling with swift, cold dread.

*T*he electric beasts had finished their pleasure. The dead were cinders on the rock. The living had run back into the tunnels. And now the blue sea of fire was flowing again, straight toward the place where they stood.

It was flowing fast, and Gray sensed an urgency, an impersonal haste, as though a command had been laid upon those living ropes of flame.

The first dim rumble of thunder rolled down the wind. Gripping Jill, Gray turned up the tunnel.

The wind, compressed in that narrow throat of rock, beat them blind and breathless, beat them to their bellies, to crawl. How long it took them, they never knew.

But Gray caught glimpses of Dio the Martian crawling behind them, and behind him again, the relentless flow of the fire-things.

They floundered out onto a rocky slope, fell away beneath the suck of the wind, and lay still, gasping. It was hot. Thunder crashed abruptly, and lightning flared between the cliffs.

Gray felt a contracting of the heart. There were no cables.

Then he saw it — the small, fast fighter flying below them on a flat plateau. A cave mouth beside it had been closed with a plastic door. The ship was the one that had followed them. He guessed at another one behind the protecting door.

Raking the tumbled blond hair out of his eyes, Gray got up.

Jill was still sitting, her black curls bowed between her hands. There wasn't much time, but Gray yielded to impulse. Pulling her head back by the silken hair, he kissed her.

"If you ever get tired of virtue, sweetheart, look me up." But somehow he wasn't grinning, and he ran down the slope.

He was almost to the open lock of the ship when things began to happen. Dio staggered out of the wind-tunnel and sagged down beside Jill. Then, abruptly, the big door opened.

Five men came out — one in pilot's costume, two in nondescript apparel, one in expensive business clothes, and the fifth in dark prison garb.

Gray recognized the last two. Caron of Mars and the errant Ward.

They were evidently on the verge of leaving. But they looked cheerful. Caron's sickly-sweet face all but oozed honey, and Ward was grinning his rat's grin.

Thunder banged and rolled among the rocks. Lightning flared in the cloudy murk. Gray saw the hull of a second ship beyond the door. Then the newcomers had seen him, and the two on the slope.

Guns ripped out of holsters. Gray's heart began to pound slowly. He, and Jill and Dio, were caught on that naked slope, with the flood of electric death at their backs.

His Indianesque face hardened. Bullets whined round him as he turned back up the slope, but he ran doubled over, putting all his hope in the tricky, uncertain light.

Jill and the Martian crouched stiffly, not knowing where to turn. A flare of lightning showed Gray the first of the firethings, flowing out onto the ledge, hidden from the men below.

"Back into the cave!" he yelled. His urgent hand fairly lifted Dio. The Martian glared at him, then obeyed. Bullets snarled against the rock. The light was too bad for accurate shooting, but luck couldn't stay with them forever.

Gray glanced over his shoulder as they scrambled up on the ledge. Caron waited by his ship. Ward and the others were charging the slope. Gray's teeth gleamed in a cruel grin.

Sweeping Jill into his arms, he stepped into the lapping flow of fire. Dio swore viciously, but he followed. They started toward the cave mouth, staggering in the rush of the wind.

"For God's sake, don't fall," snapped Gray. "Here they come!"

The pilot and one of the nondescript men were the first over. They were into the river of fire before they knew, it, and then it was too late. One collapsed and was buried. The pilot fell backward, and then other man died under his body, of a broken neck.

Ward stopped. Gray could see his face, dark and hard and calculating. He studied Gray and Dio, and the dead men. He turned and looked back at Caron. Then, deliberately, he stripped off his gun belt, threw down his gun, and waded into the river.

Gray remembered, then, that Ward too wore rubber boots, and had no metal on him.

*W*ard came on, the glowing ropes sliding surflike around his boots. Very carefully. Gray handed Jill to Dio.

"If I die too," he said, "there's only Caron down there. He's too fat to stop you."

Jill spoke, but he turned his back. He was suddenly confused, and it was almost pleasant to be able to lose his confusion in fighting. Ward had stopped some five feet away. Now he untied the length of tough cord that served him for a belt.

Gray nodded. Ward would try to throw a twist around his ankle and trip him. Once his body touched those swarming creatures. . . .

He tensed, watchfully. The rat's grin was set on Ward's dark face. The cord licked out.

But it caught Gray's throat instead of his ankle!

Ward laughed and braced himself. Cursing, Gray caught at the rope. But friction held it, and Ward pulled, hard. His face purpling, Gray could still commend Ward's strategy. In taking Gray off guard, he'd more than made up what he lost in point of leverage.

Letting his body go with the pull, Gray flung himself at Ward. Blood blinded him, his heart was pounding, but he thought he foresaw Ward's next move. He let himself be pulled almost within striking distance.

Then, as Ward stepped, aside, jerking the rope and thrusting out a tripping foot, Gray made a catlike shift of balance and bent over.

His hands almost touched that weird, flowing surf as they clasped Ward's boot. Throwing all his strength into the lift, he hurled Ward backward.

Ward screamed once and disappeared under the blue fire. Gray clawed the rope from his neck. And then, suddenly, the world began to sway under him. He knew he was falling.

Someone's hand caught him, held him up. Fighting down his vertigo as his breath came back, he saw that it was Jill.

"Why?" he gasped, but her answer was lost in a titanic roar of thunder. Lightning blasted down. Dio's voice reached him, thin and distant through the clamor.

"We'll be killed! These damn things will attract the bolts!"

It was true. All his work had been for nothing. Looking up into that low, angry sky, Gray knew he was going to die.

Quite irrelevantly, Jill's words in the tunnel came back to him. "You're a fool . . . lost truth . . . not true to lie!"

Now, in this moment, she couldn't lie to him. He caught her shoulders cruelly, trying to read her eyes.

Very faintly through the uproar, he heard her. "I'm sorry for you, Gray. Good man, gone to waste."

Dio stifled a scream. Thunder crashed between the sounding boards of the cliffs. Gray looked up.

A titanic bolt of lightning shot down, straight for them. The burning blue surf was agitated, sending up pseudopods uncannily like worshipping arms. The bolt struck.

The air reeked of ozone, but Gray felt no shock. There was a hiss, a vast stirring of creatures around him. The blue light glowed, purpled.

Another bolt struck down, and another, and still they were not dead. The fire-things had become a writhing, joyous tangle of tenuous bodies, glowing bright and brighter.

Stunned, incredulous, the three humans stood. The light was now an eye-searing violet. Static electricity tingled through them in eerie waves. But they were not burned.

"My God," whispered Gray. "They eat it. They eat lightning!"

Not daring to move, they stood watching that miracle of alien life, the feeding of living things on raw current. And when the last bolt had struck, the tide turned and rolled back down the wind-tunnel, a blinding river of living light.

Silently, the three humans went down the rocky slope to where Caron of Mars cowered in the silver ship. No bolt had come near it. And now Caron came to meet them.

His face was pasty with fear, but the old cunning still lurked in his eyes.

"Gray," he said. "I have an offer to make."

"Well?"

"You killed my pilot," said Caron suavely. "I can't fly, myself. Take me off, and I'll pay you anything you want."

"In bullets," retorted Gray. "You won't want witnesses to this."

"Circumstances force me. Physically, you have the advantage."

Jill's fingers caught his arm. "Don't, Gray! The Project. . . ."

Caron faced her. "The Project is doomed in any case. My men carried out my secondary instructions. All the cables in your valley have been cut. There is a storm now ready to break.

"In fifteen minutes or so, everything will be destroyed, except the domes. Regrettable, but. . . ." He shrugged.

Jill's temper blazed, choking her so that she could hardly speak.

"Look at him, Gray," she whispered. "That's what you're so proud of being. A cynic, who believes in nothing but himself. Look at him!"

Gray turned on her.

"Damn you!" he grated. "Do you expect me to believe you, with the world full of hypocrites like him?"

Her eyes stopped him. He remembered Moulton, pleading for her life. He remembered how she had looked back there at the tunnel, when they had been sure of death. Some of his assurance was shaken.

"Listen," he said harshly. "I can save your valley. There's a chance in a million of coming out alive. Will you die for what you believe in?"

She hesitated, just for a second. Then she looked at Dio and said, "Yes."

Gray turned. Almost lazily, his fist snapped up and took Caron on his flabby jaw.

"Take care of him, Dio," he grunted. Then he entered the ship, herding the white-faced girl before him.

*T*he ship hurtled up into airless space, where the blinding sunlight lay in sharp shadows on the rock. Over the ridge and down again, with the Project hidden under a surf of storm-clouds.

Cutting in the air motors, Gray dropped. Black, bellowing darkness swallowed them. Then he saw the valley, with the copper cables fallen, and the wheat already on fire in several places.

Flying with every bit of his skill, he sought the narrowest part of the valley and flipped over in a racking loop. The stern tubes hit rock. The nose slammed down on the opposite wall, wedging the ship by sheer weight.

Lightning gathered in a vast javelin and flamed down upon them. Jill flinched and caught her breath. The flame hissed along the hull and vanished into seared and blackened rock.

"Still willing to die for principle?" asked Gray brutally.

She glared at him. "Yes," she snapped. "But I hate having to die in your company!"

She looked down at the valley. Lightning struck with monotonous regularity on the hull, but the valley was untouched. Jill smiled, though her face was white, her body rigid with waiting.

It was the smile that did it. Gray looked at her, her tousled black curls, the lithe young curves of throat and breast. He leaned back in his seat, scowling out at the storm.

"Relax," he said. "You aren't going to die."

She turned on him, not daring to speak. He went on, slowly.

"The only chance you took was in the landing. We're acting as lightning rod for the whole valley, being the highest and best conductor. But, as a man named Faraday proved, the charge resides on the surface of the conductor. We're perfectly safe."

"How dared you!" she whispered.

He faced her, almost angrily.

"You knocked the props out from under my philosophy. I've had enough hypocritical eyewash. I had to prove you. Well, I have."

She was quiet for some time. Then she said, "I understand, Duke. I'm glad. And now what, for you?"

He shrugged wryly.

"I don't know. I can still take Caron's other ship and escape. But I don't think I want to. I think perhaps I'll stick around and give virtue another whirl."

Smoothing back his sleek fair hair, he shot her a sparkling look from under his hands.

"I won't," he added softly, "even mind going to Sunday School, if you were the teacher."